PUFFIN BOOKS

THE HICCUPS AT NO. 13

Disaster strikes one Sunday morning in the Brown family's kitchen, when Hamlet has the hiccups. His hiccuping causes some very unfortunate accidents, which *he* thinks are funny, but his mum and dad are not so amused. Dad tries a famous 'hiccup cure', but neither that nor a visit to the doctor can stop Hamlet's hiccups.

Sister Susan is fed up with all her brother's disasters, but when she makes a successful début as an actress, she has only one person to thank – Hamlet and his hiccups.

Gyles Brandreth is the author of many books of quizzes, puzzles, games and jokes. He has also written another Hamlet Brown adventure, *The Ghost at No. 13*. He is a well-known television personality and lives in London with his family.

Other books by Gyles Brandreth

THE DO-IT-YOURSELF GENIUS KIT
THE EMERGENCY JOKE KIT
THE GHOST AT NO. 13
JOKE BOX
WORD BOX

GYLES BRANDRETH

THE HICCUPS AT
No. 13

ILLUSTRATED BY JULIE TENNENT

PUFFIN BOOKS

PUFFIN BOOKS

Published by the Penguin Group
27 Wrights Lane, London W8 5TZ, England
Viking Penguin Inc., 40 West 23rd Street, New York, New York 10010, USA
Penguin Books Australia Ltd, Ringwood, Victoria, Australia
Penguin Books Canada Ltd, 2801 John Street, Markham, Ontario, Canada L3R 1B4
Penguin Books (NZ) Ltd, 182–190 Wairau Road, Auckland 10, New Zealand

Penguin Books Ltd, Registered Offices: Harmondsworth, Middlesex, England

First published by Viking Kestrel 1987
Published in Puffin Books 1988
10 9 8 7 6 5 4 3 2

Made and printed in Great Britain by
Richard Clay Ltd, Bungay, Suffolk
Filmset in Monophoto Palatino

1. A Chapter of Accidents

Hamlet Orlando Julius Caesar Brown had a problem. And it wasn't his name. It was the hiccups. Hamlet had the hiccups and he had them very badly.

Hiccuping Hamlet was nine years old and lived at No. 13 Irving Terrace, Hammersmith, West London, with his mother and father and his eleven-year-old sister Susan, who was a bit of a goodie-goodie and never had the hiccups.

This was lucky for Susan, because the noise of the hiccups was a noise that Mrs Brown found particularly irritating. It was

the sort of annoying noise that always put her in a bad mood and usually gave her one of her headaches.

'Oh do stop hiccupping, Hamlet,' said Mrs Brown in one of her crosser voices, as she handed her son a plate piled high with bacon, mushrooms and baked beans. It was Sunday morning, the first Sunday morning of the summer holidays, and Mrs Brown had made a special breakfast.

'I can't — hic — help it!' said Hamlet, looking sorry for himself and tucking into his breakfast at the same time.

'You've got the hiccups because you eat too quickly,' said Mrs Brown sternly.

'No I don't!' hiccupped Hamlet with a very full mouth.

'Yes you do,' said Mrs Brown. 'You gobble your food, you talk with your mouth full and you don't sit properly at the table.'

Mouth full or not, Hamlet would have

told his mother she was being horribly
unfair if, at that precise moment, the chair
he was leaning back on had not slipped
from under him and brought the boy and
his breakfast crashing to the floor.

Susan almost laughed, but managed to
stop herself. She carried on eating her
breakfast quietly as if nothing had
happened. Hamlet almost cried, but
managed to stop himself. Mrs Brown said
nothing, but shook her head and sighed a
very big sigh as she got out the dustpan

and brush, got down on to her hands and
knees and began to help Hamlet pick up the
bits and pieces of broken plate.

Just then the kitchen door opened and in
came a very sleepy Mr Brown. Unhappily
he did not notice his wife and son kneeling
on the floor, so that as he came through the

door he fell right over them – crash, bang, wallop!

This time Susan did burst out laughing. Hamlet thought it was rather funny too. Mrs Brown, on the other hand, was not amused.

'You numskull, why can't you look where you're going?!' she shouted at her husband, who was lying flat on his face beside her.

'I'm so sorry, dearest one,' said Mr Brown, apologetically. 'I just didn't expect to find anyone on all fours by the kitchen door at nine o'clock on Sunday morning.'

He struggled to his feet and helped Mrs Brown on to hers. 'Are you all right, dearest one?' he asked.

'I've got a splitting headache, but apart from that I'm fine,' said Mrs Brown, dusting herself down. 'Are you all right?'

'Oh yes, dear heart, no problem! I went to drama school after all. Theatre folk are *trained* to take a tumble. We know *exactly* how to fall over and not get hurt. Never forget, I am an actor!'

No one ever could forget that Mr Brown was an actor, because he always walked and talked – and fell over – as if he was on stage in the middle of an extraordinary play, even when he was only in the kitchen in the middle of an ordinary breakfast.

Mrs Brown had also been to drama school, but she didn't behave in an actressy way when she was at home. She liked being an actress – and she was a good actress – but she believed that the place for acting was the theatre or the television studio, not the kitchen at No. 13 Irving Terrace.

Mr Brown, on the other hand, couldn't help being theatrical wherever he was and all the time. 'But tell me, O queen of my heart,' he asked his wife dramatically, 'what on earth were you and young Prince Hamlet doing on the floor when I came in?'

'Tell your father what happened,' said

Mrs Brown with a frown, as she emptied
the broken bits of plate out of the dustpan
into the waste bin.

'Hic!' said Hamlet, who was now sitting
at the breakfast table with all four of the
feet of his chair planted firmly and squarely
on the floor. 'Hic!'

'Go on,' said Mrs Brown.

'Hic! I had a bit of an accident.'

'Go on,' said Mr Brown.

Susan said nothing. She was still eating
her breakfast. She never rushed it. She never
talked with her mouth full. And she never,
ever, *ever* fell off her chair.

'Well, hic,' said Hamlet, 'I was holding
my breakfast in one hand like this.' And he
picked up the butter dish to demonstrate.
'And I was holding my fork in my other
hand like this.' And he picked up a teaspoon
to show his father what he meant. 'And I
was leaning back on my chair like this,
when all of a sudden I hiccupped and –'

And, believe it or not, all of a sudden Hamlet hiccupped again and the chair slipped from under him again and the unfortunate boy and the unfortunate butter dish crashed to the floor.

This time, everybody burst out laughing — even Mrs Brown. Luckily the butter dish didn't break, and there was very little butter in it anyway. Luckily too, Hamlet wasn't hurt.

'Well, young man, I hope you've learnt your lesson. In future sit properly at the table at all times.'

'I will, Mum,' said Hamlet from the floor. 'I promise. Hic.'

2. A Cure for the Hiccups

The Sunday morning when Hamlet
happened to have the hiccups was an
unusual Sunday morning at No. 13 Irving
Terrace, because it was a Sunday morning
when the Browns were going to church.

As a rule the Browns didn't go to church
except at Christmas and Easter, but they
were going today because the local church
was having a special service for Cubs,
Brownies, Scouts and Guides, and Susan
was a Guide and a very keen Guide too.

Hamlet was too young to be a Scout, but
he had been a Cub for a time — for a very
short time. When he joined the Cubs he
thought it might be fun, but after about a
month (it was actually the week after Mrs

Brown had bought him the expensive Cubs uniform) he decided he wasn't interested after all and gave it up.

'What's so — hic — special about this service anyway?' Hamlet asked his sister grumpily, as the pair of them were clearing away the breakfast things.

'I'm reading the Lesson,' said Susan.

'Hic! It's bad enough having to go to a service without having lessons when you get there,' said Hamlet, who liked the idea of going to church about as much as he liked the idea of going to school.

'Don't be daft,' said Susan, 'it's not a lesson like at school. A Lesson at church is a reading from the Bible, and I'm the one who's doing the reading.'

'Aren't you a clever-clogs, then?' said Hamlet rather rudely – and, since his parents were hidden behind the pages of the Sunday newspapers and couldn't see him, he stuck his tongue out at his sister.

'I didn't ask to read the Lesson,' said Susan. 'Our Guider asked me if I would and I couldn't very well say no to her, could I?'

'Bet she only asked you because you suck up to her,' said Hamlet, who, though he wouldn't have admitted it to anyone, was secretly a little jealous of the fact that his sister had been asked to read out loud from

the Bible in front of hundreds of people.
He'd have quite liked to be asked himself.

'I don't suck up to anybody,' said Susan.

'You do – do – do!' said Hamlet, sticking
his tongue out again and hiccupping at the
same time.

'Now stop it, you two,' said Mr Brown,
putting down his newspaper.

'Sorry, Dad,' said Susan.

'Hic,' said Hamlet.

'And do stop hiccupping, Hamlet,' said
Mrs Brown sharply, putting down her
newspaper and getting up. 'I don't know
how we're going to be able to take you to
the service if you're going to hiccup all the
way through it.'

'Hic! Hic! Hic!' went Hamlet as loudly
and as quickly as he could. 'Hic! Hic! Hic!'
'If only the hiccups get worse,' he thought,
'I might be able to get out of this rotten
church outing altogether.'

'Don't worry about those hiccups,' said

Mr Brown. 'I know how to cure the hiccups.'

'That's a relief,' said Mrs Brown.

'That's a pity,' thought Hamlet, who had now decided that to have his hiccups cured was absolutely and utterly and completely the last thing he wanted to have happen to him.

'Oh yes,' said Mr Brown, 'my method never fails.'

'I'm pleased to hear it,' said Mrs Brown. 'Susan and I are just going upstairs to get ready and we'll leave you two to sort out the hiccups. And you'd better be quick about it. Whatever happens, we mustn't be late.'

'It's very simple, my boy,' said Mr Brown once his wife and daughter were out of the room. 'All you have to do is put your hands behind your head like this and hold your breath.'

'Hic,' said Hamlet. 'For how long?'

'For as long as it takes,' said Mr Brown.

'But isn't that dangerous?' asked Hamlet, hiccupping violently.

'I don't think so,' said Mr Brown. 'Let's have a go and see.'

'Oh no,' said Hamlet, looking anxious. 'I think it's too risky. A boy in my class once held his breath for a minute and his face went all red and his eyes nearly popped out of his head and he looked *terrible.* I'm sorry, Dad, I'd like to cure my hiccups – I would – I really would – hic – but your method sounds far too dangerous to me.'

'Never mind,' said Mr Brown. 'I do have a second method.'

'Oh no!' thought Hamlet. 'Oh yes?' he said.

'Yes,' said Mr Brown. 'It's a bit more complicated and I haven't tried it in years, but I expect it still works. What you have to do is drink a glass of water from the wrong side and the wrong way up.'

'Pardon?' said Hamlet, who knew his

father had some odd ideas but thought this sounded odder than most.

'You fill up a glass with water and then, instead of drinking it in the normal way, you bend right over it so that your head is upside down and you are trying to drink from the side of the glass that's opposite the side you'd expect to drink from – if you see what I mean.'

Hamlet did see what Mr Brown meant – just – and, since he was one hundred per cent certain that his father's amazing hiccup-cure would never work, he said he'd have a go.

Mr Brown got out a glass, filled it with water and gave it to Hamlet. Hamlet took the glass, stood up, bent his head right over it, opened his mouth to take his first sip and hiccupped – a real hiccup and a mighty one – so real and so mighty, in fact, that the shock of it quite surprised poor Hamlet, and, before he knew what had happened, the glass had slipped out of his hand and crashed to the ground.

Water and splinters of broken glass were *everywhere*.

'Odds bodkins,' cried Mr Brown, appalled at the sight of the shattered glass. 'What have we done?'

'I think we've cured my hiccups,' said

Hamlet sadly. And sure enough they had. The shock of the crashing glass seemed to have frightened the hiccups away.

'Well, that's the good news,' said Mr Brown. 'The bad news is we've broken one of your mother's favourite glasses into the bargain.'

'We'd better clear it up, then, before Mum comes down.'

'By jove, you're right. No time to be lost.'

Mr Brown got the dustpan and brush, and Hamlet got a large sheet of newspaper. Very carefully they got down on to their knees and Hamlet began to pick up the larger pieces of broken glass and put them on to the newspaper, while Mr Brown brushed the little splinters into the dustpan. They worked as quickly as they could, Mr Brown desperately hoping that they would have everything cleared up before his wife came in and Hamlet desperately hoping that

somehow his hiccups would return. Both of
them were to be desperately disappointed.

Just as they had finished the job and
were about to scramble to their feet, the
kitchen door opened and in walked Mrs
Brown. Unfortunately she did not notice her
husband and son on all fours on the floor,

so as she came into the room she fell head over heels on top of them.

'Ooops, sorry, Mum,' said Hamlet.

'Oh my dearest one,' said Mr Brown jumping up and hauling his wife to her feet, 'Are you all right, my precious?'

'Yes, I'm fine, thank you very much,' said Mrs Brown through clenched teeth. 'I'm an actress, don't forget. I went to drama school. I've been trained to take a tumble!'

3. Get Me to the Church on Time

The special service they were going to was
due to begin at eleven o'clock – on the dot.
Mrs Brown had wanted everybody out of
the house and on their way to the church
by 10.00 a.m. – *sharp.* In the event it was
nearly twenty-five to eleven before the
Browns were in the car and on the road –
and none of them was in a very good
mood.

Mrs Brown was cross with Mr Brown for
tripping her up in the kitchen. Mr Brown
was cross with Hamlet Brown for dropping
one of Mrs Brown's favourite glasses.
Hamlet Brown was cross with Mrs Brown
for telling him off and with Mr Brown for

curing his hiccups and with Susan Brown
for being a ghastly goodie-goodie who
never got the hiccups and never broke
anything and was always everybody's
favourite.

For once, even Susan Brown was cross.
She was cross because she thought she was
going to be late for the service and you
don't want to be late for a service when
you are going to be reading the Lesson at
it — at least Susan Brown didn't want to
be.

'Don't worry, my little princess,' said Mr
Brown as he swerved the car out of Irving
Terrace and into the main road. 'We'll get
you to the church on time.' As he spoke he
suddenly noticed a little red light flickering
on the car dashboard. He very much hoped
nobody else would notice it. Unfortunately
somebody did — Mrs Brown.

'What's that red light on for?' she yelped,
already knowing the answer.

'Nothing, dearest,' said Mr Brown, trying to sound as casual as possible.

'Exactly — *nothing!*' shrieked Mrs Brown. 'It means there's nothing left in the petrol tank, doesn't it?'

'Well, not quite, my sweet,' said Mr Brown, doing his best to sound as cool as a cucumber when he was beginning to feel as hot as an Indian curry. 'It means there's *almost* nothing left in the petrol tank — but I'm absolutely sure there is enough left to get us to the church.' Mr Brown wasn't absolutely sure at all. He crossed his fingers, pressed his foot down on the accelerator and hoped for the best. The car sped on.

'We'll never make it now,' growled Mrs Brown. She was furious. Poor Susan was very worried. Hamlet, of course, was delighted. He didn't want to go to a boring old service to listen to his boring old sister reading some boring old bit from the Bible. If he couldn't have the hiccups and get out of it that way, the car having a breakdown was just as good.

'I told you to go to the garage yesterday,' Mrs Brown scolded her husband. 'We're going to run out of petrol in the middle of the main road, you mark my words!'

No sooner had she spoken than the car screeched to a halt.

'There you are!' said Mrs Brown, almost triumphantly. 'What did I tell you?'

Susan burst into tears.

'It's a red light,' said Mr Brown.

'I know it's a red light,' said Mrs Brown. 'I can see it's a red light. It's a red light telling us we've run out of petrol, you dunderhead!'

'No, no, no,' said Mr Brown, 'not that little red light – the big red traffic light. I've stopped because we're at the traffic lights and they're red.'

'Oh,' said Mrs Brown, who couldn't really think of anything else to say.

The lights turned to amber and then to green and the car moved off again.

'I think we'll have enough petrol to get us to the church,' said Mr Brown, 'just.' And they did. Just.

They arrived as the church clock was striking eleven. They rushed up the path and into the church as fast as their feet would carry them. The congregation was just starting to sing the first hymn and the vicar and the choir and the Mayor and Mayoress of Hammersmith and the parade of Cubs and Brownies and Scouts and Guides were about to make their way down the aisle from the back of the church to the front. In the nick of time Susan was able to join the other Guides.

The church was jam-packed full. The Browns couldn't see anywhere to sit, except right at the front. Mrs Brown wanted to stand at the back, but Mr Brown whispered to Mrs Brown that since there were three free seats at the front it seemed a pity to waste them – so Mr Brown, Mrs Brown and Hamlet tagged themselves on to the end of the procession and made their way to the front of the church where they sat in the three empty seats that had, in fact, been specially reserved for the Mayor, the Mayoress and the Mayor's Mace Bearer.

Though the Mayor and his party were right at the front of the procession they were the last to take their seats, because they had to stand at the front of the church looking important until everybody else was seated. When they came to sit down themselves, they found the Browns in their places, but it was too late to ask them to move (and they were too polite anyway) so that the Mayor, the Mayoress and the Mayor's Mace Bearer squeezed up with Mr Brown, Mrs Brown and Hamlet and the six of them sat there squashed into the front row like very fat sardines in a very small tin.

It wasn't at all comfortable and it wasn't much fun. The service seemed to go on and on and on. And on. There were hymns, there were prayers, there was a very long sermon from the vicar, and there were the Lessons — not just one, as Hamlet had expected, but four in all. A Cub read the

first one, followed by a Brownie, followed
by a Scout, followed, at long, long last, by
Susan.

When her turn came, Susan got up and
moved to the beautiful brass lectern shaped
like a flying eagle that stood in front of the

altar. She took up her position, looked out at the congregation — there really were hundreds of people there — swallowed hard, breathed deeply and began to read.

She read clearly, she read loudly, she read *beautifully*. But when she was halfway through, something unexpected happened. From the front row came a different loud, clear, not at all beautiful but quite unmistakable sound: 'Hic!'

It was Hamlet and he had the hiccups.

'Sshh!' went Mr Brown.

'Sshh! Sshh!' went Mrs Brown.

'Sshh! Sshh! Ssshh!' went the Mayor.

'Hic!' went Hamlet.

Susan went on reading, as loudly and clearly and beautifully as ever. Hamlet went on hiccupping, and, as the seconds ticked slowly by, his hiccups seemed to get louder and louder and louder. He wasn't doing it on purpose — he wasn't, he really wasn't. He wanted to stop — he did, he really did.

But unfortunately for Hamlet (and unfortunately for Susan) you just can't control the hiccups. And that's a fact.

4. Susan Brown, Superstar

The following morning Hamlet was still in disgrace. And he still had the hiccups.

'What do you say to your sister?' Mrs Brown asked him as soon as he came into the kitchen for breakfast.

'Hic. Sorry,' said Hamlet, and, for once, he meant it.

'It doesn't matter,' said Susan. And she meant it too. What's more, she was right. Hamlet's hiccupping in church hadn't mattered all that much. At the time it had seemed horribly loud to Susan and to Mrs Brown and Mr Brown – and the Mayor – but, in fact, hardly anybody else in the church had noticed it, and when the service was over and everybody was leaving the vicar came over to the Browns, not to complain about Hamlet's hiccupping but to congratulate Susan on her beautiful reading.

Susan knew that yesterday's reading had been a success, so that today she was in a happy mood and ready to forgive her hiccupping younger brother. But even if Sunday's reading hadn't gone so well, Susan would still have been in a good mood by Monday morning, because this Monday morning was a special Monday morning.

It was a Monday morning on which Susan knew she was going to see a dream come true, because today Miss Susan Brown of No. 13 Irving Terrace, Hammersmith, West London, was going to become an actress — yes, a genuine actress appearing in a proper play.

Hamlet had no idea what he was going to be when he grew up. Some days he thought he might quite like to be the first person from Hammersmith to land on the moon. Other days he thought he'd like to be a vet – or a surgeon – or a snooker player – or an airline pilot – or a multi-millionaire who didn't do anything but lie in bed all day watching TV and eating chocolate ice-cream.

From the age of seven Susan had wanted to be an actress and she had no doubts about the matter at all. She had always had the star part in the Brownie shows (the Jester's badge was the first badge she got) and she had been in the school nativity play five years running – first as a sheep, then as a shepherd, next as a Wise Man, then as Mary, and finally as the Archangel Gabriel. (Hamlet thought she was particularly soppy as the angel.)

But the play she was going to be in now was something different: it was a real play with real actors being put on in a real theatre for real audiences to pay real money to come and see. To be frank, the reason Susan had a part in the play wasn't that she was the world's greatest actress. It was because her father had a part in the play as well.

The play was being staged at the Open Air Theatre in London's Regent's Park. It was called *Noah* and, as you might guess, it was about Noah and his Ark. Mr Brown didn't have the main part (he was rather cross about that, as a matter of fact), but he had a very good part nonetheless. He was playing a character called Ham, one of Noah's three sons, and Susan was going to play the part of Ham's small daughter, one of Noah's many grandchildren. Susan wasn't going to play the part at every performance —she had to take it in turns with the producer's ten-year-old daughter, Naomi — and it was a very small part indeed — she was only going to be on stage for five minutes — but it was still thrilling for Susan, and of course, she was very, *very* excited about it.

'When do you – hic – come on?' asked Hamlet, who felt he ought to show a little interest, even though he was secretly disappointed that in the play Noah had only granddaughters and no grandsons.

'Right at the end,' said Susan, 'with the animals!'

'With the animals? Are they having actors dressed up as animals, then?' asked Hamlet, thinking that perhaps there might be room for him as a monkey or a lion.

'Oh no,' said Susan. 'They're using real animals.'

'Hic! – I don't believe it,' said Hamlet.

''Tis true,' said Mr Brown. 'The Open Air Theatre is right by the zoo, so we're using real animals in the play. They're coming in two by two . . .'

'And I'm calling out their names and ticking them off on a list as they arrive,' said Susan proudly.

'It's an amazing A to Z of birds and

beasts,' explained Mr Brown, 'from aardvarks to zebras!'

'What's an aardvark?' asked Hamlet.

'Everyone knows what an aardvark is,' said Susan.

'Well, I don't,' said Hamlet, who had never heard of an aardvark before and didn't much like the sound of it now.

'It's a large burrowing animal with very big ears and a very heavy tail and a very, very long tongue.'

'Hic! – what's it use its tongue for?' asked Hamlet, who thought the aardvark sounded like a dangerous cross between an elephant and a rattlesnake.

'For eating ants with,' said Susan.

'Ugh,' said Hamlet. 'How disgusting! And there's going to be a real live aardvark in your play?'

'Two of them, actually,' said Mr Brown. 'There're going to be two of each of the different kinds of animal — fifty in all.'

'There ought to be — hic — fifty-two if it's going to be a complete A to Z,' said Hamlet smartly.

'The people at the zoo couldn't think of an animal beginning with x,' said Mr Brown.

'Can you?' said Susan.

Hamlet couldn't, of course, so all he said was 'Hic!' and got on with eating his breakfast.

5. The Best Medicine

After breakfast Mr Brown took Susan off to the Open Air Theatre in Regent's Park for her first rehearsal, and Mrs Brown took Hamlet off to the doctor. He was still hiccupping as noisily as ever, and Mrs Brown thought it was high time something was done about it.

Mrs Brown and Hamlet sat in the doctor's waiting-room for almost an hour before the doctor could see them. Hamlet hiccupped non-stop and by the time the pair of them got into the doctor's surgery Hamlet's mother had such a headache she felt she was the one who should be seeing the doctor, not Hamlet.

'Now what seems to be the problem?'

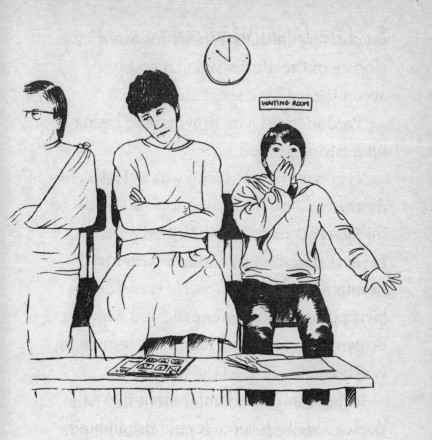

asked Dr Lo when, at long last, the Browns
were seated in front of her.

'Hamlet has the hiccups,' said Mrs
Brown.

'Hic!' said Hamlet, trying to be helpful.

'I see,' said Dr Lo, 'a spasmodic

involuntary inhalation of air followed by closure of the glottis simultaneously accompanied by a short sharp click.'

'Pardon?' said Mrs Brown, who hadn't understood a word.

'Hic!' said Hamlet, who was as lost as his mother.

'Exactly,' said Dr Lo. 'Nothing serious. Does he eat too fast and talk with his mouth full?'

'Yes,' said Mrs Brown.

'No,' said Hamlet.

'I thought so,' said the doctor.

'What can you do about it?' asked Mrs Brown, whose head was now throbbing in time with Hamlet's hiccupping.

'Not a lot,' said Dr Lo, looking somewhat solemn. 'The symptoms can generally be controlled by deep inhalations of carbon dioxide and only if they persist would one consider the possibility of resorting to a course of chlorpromazine.'

'Pardon?' said Mrs Brown, who was more confused than ever.

'Hic!' said Hamlet, who thought the Chinese doctor was talking double Dutch.

'Of course,' said Dr Lo, 'he could always try standing on his head.'

'What?' said Mrs Brown, not quite believing her ears.

'It sometimes works,' continued the doctor, looking more serious than ever. 'You see, the cause of the hiccup is irritation of the nerves that go to the diaphragm and produce these spasmodic contractions – and taking a deep breath and standing on your head sometimes sorts it out.'

Hamlet didn't have a clue what the doctor was burbling on about, but he just about grasped the fact that she wanted him to stand on his head, so, thinking, 'the sooner I get on with it the sooner we'll be out of here', he got down on his hands and knees, took a deep breath and there and then, right in front of the doctor's desk, swung his legs into the air.

'Well done!' said Dr Lo.

'Goodness gracious me!' said Mrs Brown.

'Hic!' said Hamlet, and, as he hiccupped, a dreadful thing happened: he toppled over! His whole upside-down body wobbled for a moment and then – crash! bang! wallop!

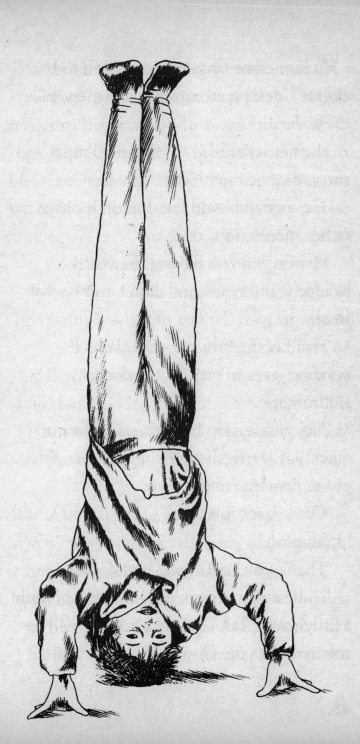

– his legs came smashing down on to the doctor's desk, scattering pens, papers, pills, *everywhere*.

Hamlet scrambled to his feet. 'I'm so sorry, hic,' he mumbled.

'Never mind,' said the doctor, looking sad rather than serious now.

Mrs Brown was having the worst headache of her life and didn't know what to say.

'Hic! Let me tidy up,' said Hamlet, bending over to pick up the doctor's stethoscope.

'No, please, don't worry,' said the doctor quickly. Clearly she felt she had seen enough of the Browns for one day.

'Come back in a week's time if you're still hiccupping.'

'Thank you,' muttered Mrs Brown.

'I'll be away myself,' said the doctor with a little smile, 'but I'm sure Dr Perry will be able to help you. Goodbye.'

Dr Lo opened the door for Mrs Brown and Hamlet, who picked their way across the littered floor and hurried out of the surgery as rapidly as their legs would carry them.

When they got back to No. 13 Irving Terrace, they found that Mr Brown and Susan were already home and having lunch. Unlike the visit to the doctor, the rehearsal at the Open Air Theatre had been a huge success. Susan was very excited.

'They've built an enormous Noah's Ark right in the middle of the stage,' she explained to Hamlet, who wasn't listening, 'and there really are going to be fifty animals coming on two by two. It's wonderful!'

'Hic! It's boring!' said Hamlet, picking up a comic and plonking himself down in a chair.

'Don't sit there!' shouted his father.

'Hamlet, get up!' screamed his sister.

Mr Brown and Susan made such a noise and so suddenly that Hamlet almost leapt out of his skin. He certainly leapt out of the chair.

'What's wrong?' he yelped.

'It's the aardvark!' said Mr Brown.

'The *what*?' gulped Hamlet.

'The baby aardvark, the one we're using in the play,' said Susan. 'We've brought it home for you to see.'

Very gently Mr Brown picked up the small bundle that Hamlet had very nearly sat on and put it on the table. Carefully he unfolded the blanket and there was the baby aardvark: the size of a tiny piglet, with large floppy ears, a heavy tail, a pointed snout and a very long, very thin tongue that kept darting in and out of its mouth. The claws on its little paws looked horribly sharp.

'Don't worry,' said Mr Brown, 'it won't eat you.'

'It only eats ants,' said Susan with a grin.

'It's a remarkable little creature,' said Mrs Brown, coming over from the sink to take a closer look. 'Apart from anything else, it knows how to cure the hiccups.'

And suddenly everybody realized that since the surprise of almost sitting on the aardvark, Hamlet hadn't hiccupped once.

'You're right,' said Hamlet happily. 'That's a relief.'

And it was.

6. 'Help! Help!'

Aardvarks are nocturnal animals: they don't like the light. So when everyone had had a good look at the strange little creature, Mr Brown wrapped it up in the blanket again and tucked it into a large cardboard box.

'It likes to sleep all day,' said Mr Brown. 'I'll put the box in a quiet corner in the hallway, then it won't be disturbed.'

'I haven't got any ants for its tea,' said Mrs Brown.

'Don't worry, I'll take it back to the park this afternoon and they'll feed it at the zoo. It'll be quite happy just snoozing till then.'

'I wouldn't mind a snooze after lunch,' said Hamlet, who, having hiccupped non-stop for a day and a half, was feeling tired.

'No you don't, young man,' said his mother firmly. 'When you've had your lunch, I want you and Susan to go to the supermarket for me.'

Hamlet groaned.

'Of course, Mum,' said Susan, smiling her sweetest smile.

Immediately after lunch Mrs Brown gave Hamlet and Susan her shopping list and a ten-pound note. 'There's quite a lot to get,' she said. 'You'd better take the basket-on-wheels. It's in the hallway. Now off you both go and don't take all day about it.'

In the hallway, on the floor right next to the basket-on-wheels, was the cardboard box containing the sleeping aardvark.

'Let's have another look at him,' said Hamlet, peering into the box and very gently pulling back the blanket. The baby aardvark wasn't asleep at all. It was looking wide-eyed, wide-awake and really rather friendly.

'Let's take him with us,' said Hamlet.

'What do you mean?' said Susan.

'Let's take the aardvark to the supermarket. Give him a ride in the basket-on-wheels. He'll love it.'

'We'd better ask Mum first,' said Susan, who wasn't sure Mrs Brown would approve.

Hamlet *knew* Mrs Brown wouldn't approve. 'She'll only say "No". Come on, Susan, don't be such a goodie-goodie.'

Susan didn't like being called a goodie-goodie by her brother. And she couldn't see that a *short* outing in the basket-on-wheels would do the baby aardvark any harm. In fact, it *would* be rather fun to give the quaint little creature a quick ride to the supermarket and back. They'd only be gone for half an hour . . . Yes, once in a while even good-as-gold Guides like to do things that are just a tiny, eany weany bit naughty. So Susan said, 'Okay!' and helped her brother lift the aardvark out of its box and into the basket-on-wheels.

The supermarket was only five minutes away from the Browns' house, but it was difficult to tell whether or not the aardvark enjoyed the ride, because it spent the whole journey curled up in the blanket at the bottom of the basket-on-wheels with its eyes shut tight.

When they got to the supermarket the shopping didn't take long. Hamlet pushed the basket-on-wheels and read out what they had to buy from Mrs Brown's list. Susan took a supermarket trolley and collected the items from the shelves. In under ten minutes they'd got everything they needed and made their way to the check-out.

The supermarket was crowded, so the queue at the check-out desk was a long one. Susan and Hamlet stood patiently in line for what seemed like an hour and a half, but

was actually six minutes. Just as they were
getting to the front of the queue something
quite startling happened: the very fat lady
who was standing immediately behind them
began to scream.

'Help! Help!' she screeched. 'Fetch the
manager!'

Susan and Hamlet and everyone else in
the queue turned in alarm to look at the
fat lady. 'Help! Help!' she went on
squawking.

'What is it?' called out the girl at the till.

'There! There! Look!' shrieked the fat
woman, pointing a shaking finger at
Hamlet's basket-on-wheels.

'What is it?' shouted the manager, who
was hurrying through the shop towards
them.

'It's a horrible, horrible creature!'

screamed the fat lady at the top of her voice.

'No, it isn't,' said Hamlet, 'it's an aardvark!'

And so it was. The little animal had obviously woken up and decided to have a quick peek at what was going on. It meant no harm. All it was doing was peering over the edge of the basket-on-wheels, blinking in the bright light and flicking its long thin tongue in and out. But the fat lady didn't know it meant no harm. What's more, even if she had heard of an aardvark, she had certainly never seen one, and now that she was seeing one she didn't much like the look of it.

All right, it was only a very small baby aardvark and she was a very large fat lady, but she was frightened. In fact, she was terrified! She screamed and screamed and screamed and, to make matters worse, when the other customers caught sight of the strange animal they began screaming too.

'It's a giant rat!' squealed a little old lady who was standing just behind the big fat lady.

'What – a rat?' cried the manager.

'No, it's an aardvark,' said Hamlet – but by then nobody could hear him. They were all too busy screaming and shouting and calling 'Help! Help! There are giant rats *everywhere!*'

All of a sudden there was chaos. A moment before the supermarket had been full of happy customers quietly going about their everyday shopping. Now the whole place was like a madhouse. The poor manager didn't know what to do, so he switched on the fire alarm.

This turned out to be a surprisingly sensible move, because the moment people heard the fire alarm they stopped screaming and rushing round in circles. They dropped their shopping and hurried out of the supermarket instead.

Susan and Hamlet – and the aardvark in
the basket-on-wheels – were among the first

to make their escape. They got out as
quickly as they could and, having decided

that there wasn't much point in trying to explain things to the manager, raced home at top speed.

At No. 13 Irving Terrace their parents were waiting for them.

'Where's the shopping?' said Mrs Brown.

'Where's the aardvark?' said Mr Brown.

When Hamlet and Susan had finished telling their story, Mr and Mrs Brown were very cross indeed, and they both blamed Hamlet.

'It wasn't really Hamlet's fault,' said Susan, which was nice of her.

'Whose fault was it, then, may I ask?' said Mr Brown, raising his eyebrows.

'Of course it's Hamlet's fault,' said Mrs Brown crossly. 'Everywhere he goes he causes chaos — first in the kitchen, then at the doctor's, and now at the supermarket. Wherever next?'

'I'm sorry, my boy,' said his father sternly, 'but enough's enough.'

'Exactly,' said Mrs Brown. 'You can go up to your room for the rest of the afternoon.'

'It's just as much my fault,' protested Susan.

'In that case,' said Mrs Brown, turning to her daughter and looking crosser than ever, 'you can stay down here and wash the dishes. And when you've done the dishes you can peel the potatoes. And the carrots.'

'And the brussels sprouts,' added Mr Brown.

'We haven't got any brussels sprouts,' snapped Mrs Brown. 'They're still at the supermarket with the rest of the shopping!'

Mr Brown shook his head and looked glum. Susan looked as if she were going to cry. Hamlet looked pretty miserable too. 'What am I supposed to do in my room?' he asked.

'I don't know,' said Mrs Brown irritably. Her headache was coming on all over again.

'I do,' said Mr Brown. 'You can write out a long list of animals, from A to Z — starting with aardvark!'

And so saying Mr Brown carefully picked the baby aardvark out of the basket-on-wheels and took it straight off to the car. He was going to drive it back to the zoo before anything else could happen to it.

'That's an excellent idea of your father's,'

said Mrs Brown (who didn't often say that about Mr Brown's ideas). 'Go to your room, Hamlet, and don't come down till you've written out that list — from A to Z.'

'Starting with aardvark,' sighed Hamlet, who couldn't for the life of him think how to spell the word.

'Exactly,' said Mrs Brown. 'And you, Susan, you stay put here till you've cleaned all those dishes and peeled all those vegetables. I'm fed up with the pair of you.'

7. From A to Z

When Mr Brown had driven off to the zoo with the baby aardvark and Mrs Brown had gone up to bed for her lie-down, poor Susan was left in the kitchen to do the chores, while poor Hamlet was sent to his room to write out his list of animals – from A to Z.

'And don't you dare come out of your room till you've finished the list,' said Mrs Brown fiercely as Hamlet passed her on the stairs. 'I'll be listening out for you.'

Hamlet knew this wasn't entirely true, because when Mrs Brown went to bed she put ear-plugs in her ears so that she wouldn't hear anything. (She also put a special eye-shade over her eyes to keep out the light. When Mrs Brown had a rest she didn't like to be disturbed.)

In his room Hamlet sat down at his small wooden desk, got out a pencil and a piece of paper and set to work. At the top of the page he wrote ARDVARK. Under that he wrote BEAR, then COW, then DOG, then ELEPHANT.

'This is easy,' he thought. 'I'll be out of here in a jiffy.'

He wrote down FROG next, then GIRRAFFE, then HORSE, then – then – then . . . 'What on earth begins with *i*?' he wondered. 'There must be *something*.'

For a minute or two Hamlet sat chewing the end of his pencil. 'There are lots beginning with *h* – there's horse and hedgehog and hippopotamus and hyena – there must be *something* beginning with *i*.'

There is, but Hamlet couldn't think of it. And he couldn't think what to do about it either. All he could think was, 'If I don't come up with an animal beginning with the letter *i*, I'll be stuck in this room for ever. I suppose a bird would do. Or a fish.'

But poor Hamlet couldn't think of an animal or a bird or a fish beginning with an *i*. Then, suddenly, he thought of his sister. 'Susan'll know! She's got a complete list of animals from A to Z for her play. I'll ask Susan.'

He rushed to his bedroom door, flung it open and was about to run downstairs to the kitchen when a voice shouted out, 'Back in that room, Hamlet!' His mother hadn't put in her ear-plugs after all.

Hamlet closed his bedroom door again. He sighed a very heavy sigh. He wanted to cry. In fact, the tears were just coming into his eyes when he had an idea – an absolutely amazingly wonderfully brilliant idea.

Hamlet rushed to his desk and scribbled a note on a piece of paper:

DEAR SUSAN,
I'M STUCK IN MY ROOM AND I NEED YOUR HELP.
WHAT'S AN ANIMAL BEGINNING WITH 'I'? THIS IS
AN EMERGENCY SO DO HELP – PLEASE.

SIGNED

YOUR DESPERATE BROTHER HAMLET

P.S. AND WHILE YOU'RE AT IT, WHAT'S AN

   ANIMAL BEGINNING WITH 'J'?

Having written the note, he took off his right shoe and tucked the note inside it. Then he took both the sheets off his bed and tied them together. Next he tied his shoe to one end of one of the sheets. Finally, and very quietly, he opened his bedroom window and, slowly and gently, he lowered the shoe on the end of the sheet out of the window.

Luckily for Hamlet, although Mrs Brown hadn't put in her ear-plugs she had put on her eye-shade, so that lying in bed she didn't see the shoe dangling from the end of the white sheet as it came down past her bedroom window.

Just as luckily for Hamlet, when the dangling shoe got down as far as the kitchen window, Susan was standing by the sink and saw it straightaway. She leant

over the sink, opened the window, reached
for the shoe, found the note and read it.

'Animals beginning with *i* and *j*? No problem!' And out of her pocket she fished the list of the animals that were going to be in the play. A moment later, on the back of Hamlet's note, she was able to write her reply:

DEAR HAMLET,

I AM HAPPY TO BE OF ASSISTANCE. THE

<u>IGUANA</u> IS A KIND OF LIZARD

AND THE <u>JACKASS</u> IS A SORT OF DONKEY.

WITH BEST WISHES FROM YOUR SISTER,

SUSAN

She popped the note back into the shoe and gave the sheet a gentle tug. Very carefully Hamlet hauled the shoe back up to his bedroom.

'An *iguana*? Never heard of it,' thought Hamlet as he copied the word down on to his list. He was about to write JACKASS underneath it when suddenly he thought of JAGUAR and, feeling mightily pleased with himself, put that down instead.

The letter *k* was easy: there was KANGAROO or KOALA or KIWI. He put down KIWI and thought how sensible he'd been to watch that TV documentary about wildlife in Australia and New Zealand last week. LION was obvious. So was MONKEY. All he could come up with for *n* was NEWT, but he reckoned it would do.

He listed three birds next: OSTRICH for *o*, PEACOCK for *p* and QUAIL for *q*. He was especially pleased to have remembered QUAIL.

Another easy one was *r*. He was going to write RHINOCEROS, but he wasn't sure where the *h* went, so he put down RABBIT instead. For *s* he listed SNAKE, for *t*, TIGER, and for *u*, UNICORN. 'Why not?' he said to himself. 'Nobody told me they had to be *real* animals.'

His list was almost complete. He wasn't one hundred per cent sure, but he *thought* a VOLE was a kind of mouse. He was a

hundred and one per cent certain a
WALLABY was a kind of kangaroo. He
knew too that he didn't have to find an
animal for x, so that only left y and z.

The letter z was no problem: ZEBRA, of
course. But what about y? He sat and he
thought. And he thought and he sat. But
sitting and thinking and thinking and sitting
didn't bring any names of animals or birds or
insects or fish beginning with the letter y into
young Hamlet's head.

He didn't want to have to ask Susan again,
but he didn't want to be stuck in his room for
ever either. Then, all of a sudden, he had a
brainwave – the dictionary. He'd look in the
dictionary. He had his own dictionary, a
special pocket dictionary Mrs Brown's sister
(Auntie Susan) had given him for Christmas.
At the time he'd thought it was rather a
boring sort of present; he'd never opened it,
in fact, but now it was exactly what he
needed.

Hamlet went to his bookshelf and got down the dictionary. 'If there's an animal beginning with *y* it's got to be here,' he thought, and he was right. He turned to the letter *y* and there it was, just after YACHT and just before YARD: 'YAK, a large long-haired long-horned ox from Tibet and the mountains of Central Asia.'

'Yippee! I've done it!' he shouted. And, with a little help from his sister and his aunt, he had.

8. 'Who's a Clever Boy, Then?'

'Who's a clever boy, then?' said Mr Brown
to his son at supper when he looked at
Hamlet's amazing A to Z of animals. 'I'm
most impressed, young man, *most*

impressed. Congratulations!'

'It was easy, really,' said Hamlet, shrugging his shoulders.

'Far from it,' said Mr Brown. 'I'm sure I'd never have come up with IGUANA.'

Hamlet grinned and winked at Susan. Susan winked back.

'Did you think putting in UNICORN was a cheat?' asked Hamlet.

'Certainly not,' declared Mr Brown, who couldn't for the life of him think of another animal that began with a *u*.

'We're having two unicorns in the play after all,' said Susan.

'Real ones?' said Hamlet, quite surprised.

'Of course not, stupid. Unicorns don't exist. We're having ponies with cardboard horns strapped on to their heads.'

'They're the only animals who don't manage to get on to the Ark,' explained Mr Brown. 'They arrive late and miss the boat. It's rather sad.'

'Is it a sad play, then?' asked Hamlet.

'Only bits of it,' said Mr Brown. 'Most of it's very jolly – as you'll see for yourself next week.'

The next seven days, the week leading up to the first performance of *Noah* at the Open Air Theatre in Regent's Park, were happy ones for the four members of the Brown family.

Mr Brown loved being an actor so much that he was always happy and excited just before the opening of a new play. Susan was happy and excited too: her part in the play was a tiny one, she only came on right at the end and all she had to do was read out the names of the animals as they were being led up into the Ark, but it was an important part (the producer said so) and it was simply wonderful to feel that she was a real actress in a real play.

Mrs Brown, of course, really was a real actress, but she didn't appear in plays very often. Her speciality was recording the voices that go with television commercials. She only recorded these 'voice-overs', as she

called them, now and again, but she was due to do one on Friday, which was good news because, though the recording session wouldn't last more than an hour, Mrs

Brown would earn a lot of money for it because she got paid again and again every time the advertisement using her voice was shown on TV.

Hamlet was happy that week as well. There was no school – no hiccups – no aardvarks – no accidents – and lots of old black-and-white comedies to watch on the box. 'This is the life!' thought Hamlet. And it was.

At twenty-five past two on the following Monday afternoon Hamlet and Mrs Brown were sitting in the very front row at the Open Air Theatre in Regent's Park waiting for the first performance of *Noah* to begin. It was a cold afternoon and dreadfully windy, but Mrs Brown and Hamlet had come prepared. They were wearing winter overcoats, they had rugs over their knees and they each had an umbrella – just in case.

Mr Brown and Susan were backstage,

dressed in their costumes, made up and
ready to go. They were both horribly
nervous, especially Susan. Mr Brown, after

all, had been in lots of real plays before. This was Susan's first and she didn't want to make any mistakes.

At half past two, on the dot, the play began — and it was very good. Hamlet was quite surprised. He had been to see his father act in several plays before and hadn't understood a word of any of them. The worst had been a play called *Hamlet*. It was Mr Brown's favourite, written by Mr Brown's favourite playwright, William Shakespeare. Mr Brown had played the main part of Hamlet in the year that Hamlet was born, which is how he got his name. Mr Brown had been in *Hamlet* again last summer, playing a much smaller part: the ghost of Hamlet's father, who was also called Hamlet! It was very confusing and didn't make any sense to Hamlet Brown at all. But this play about Noah and his Ark did make sense. It was really very interesting and Hamlet thought that Mr

Brown (wearing a long false beard) was the best thing in it.

In the play Noah had three sons: Ham, Shem and Japheth. Mr Brown played Ham, which made Hamlet think that if he'd been born this year instead of nine years ago he'd only have had half his name and been called Ham instead of Hamlet. (Hamlet was always grateful for the fact that he hadn't been born at Christmas in the year that Mr Brown played the part of Rumpelstiltskin in a pantomime.)

Halfway through the performance of *Noah* there was an interval. Even though it was so cold and wintry Hamlet asked if he could have an ice-cream — raspberry-ripple in a tub, one of his favourites. Mrs Brown felt she needed warming up, so she decided to have a cup of coffee and a hot dog. Unfortunately almost everybody else in the audience seemed to have the same idea, and poor Mrs Brown had to spend a quarter of an hour standing in the queue waiting to be served.

Just as she had taken her second mouthful of hot dog and her first gulp of coffee, the interval was over and it was time for them to go back to their seats. Mrs Brown hated hurrying her food, she was a very sensible eater (mothers usually are), but today she had no alternative: she had to gobble up the hot dog, gulp down the coffee and hurry back to her place in the theatre. After all, when you are sitting in the very front row you can't afford to be late. Besides, she and Hamlet were both looking forward to the rest of the play, especially, of course, to the very end when

Susan and the animals were going to come on.

The second half seemed to go much more quickly than the first, a good thing since the weather was getting worse and the members of the audience were really beginning to feel the cold. Because the play was about Noah's Ark and the coming of the Great Flood there was a lot of talk in it about rain. Noah and his family seemed to be expecting it to pour at any minute. Looking up at the darkening skies, so did Mrs Brown and Hamlet.

Luckily for everyone, it didn't rain.

But unluckily for Susan it *was* very windy, so windy, in fact, that when it came to Susan's Big Moment, and, as Noah's granddaughter, she stepped on to the stage to read out her list of the names of all the animals as they arrived on the Ark, a ghastly great gust of wind *blew the list clean out of her hands*! Helplessly she watched her

precious piece of paper flutter away into the
distance, blown high and fast over the
heads of the audience.

Poor Susan! What was she to do? She couldn't very well rush off the stage and start chasing the list. Anyway, there was no point: it had blown way out of sight by now. And there was no time — here were the animals, being led on, two by two. She mustn't panic. She would *pretend* to read the names off an imaginary list and just hope and pray that she remembered them all.

The baby aardvarks were brought on first. No problem: she knew them. In fact, she knew one of them personally.

'Two aardvarks,' she said in a loud clear voice and with her pencil she ticked them off on the make-believe piece of paper she was pretending to hold.

A pair of badgers were brought on next. 'Two badgers,' said Susan confidently, ticking off their names on her invisible list.

Then came a pair of cats, a pair of dogs and two emus. 'Two cats . . . two dogs . . . two emus . . .' Susan called out the names.

'Two fieldmice . . . two goats . . . two hedgehogs . . .'

Hamlet was thinking to himself what a pity it was that there weren't going to be any elephants or giraffes or hippopotamuses, when he realized that something was wrong. Two large lizard-like animals were being brought on to the stage and Susan was, well, Susan was just standing there, staring at them, not saying a word. She was simply looking at them, with her mouth open, speechless. Her mind had gone blank, totally blank! What were they? They weren't lizards – they were like lizards, but they had a special name, it began with *i*. She knew it, she knew she knew it, it was on the tip of her tongue . . . 'Two –'

Just then, from the very front row of the audience came a very odd noise.

'Hig!'

It was Hamlet hiccupping.

'Hig!'

It was Hamlet hiccupping – not a real hiccup, but a pretend hiccup and exactly the helpful hiccup Susan needed to jog her memory.

'Hig!' went Hamlet.
'Higuanas!!' said Susan.
Mrs Brown gave a huge sigh of relief.

Mr Brown, who was watching from the side of the stage, stopped chewing his false beard and grinned from ear to ear. Hamlet stopped hiccupping, folded his arms and sat back, well pleased with his afternoon's work.

From then on Susan had no difficulty remembering the names of any of the other animals. She announced each and every one of them in loud, clear, confident tones and nobody, apart from the Browns, seemed to have noticed the slight hiccup in her performance. Certainly at the end of the play, when Susan came on to take her bow, the audience cheered very loudly.

Once it was all over, Mrs Brown and Hamlet went backstage to say 'Well done' to Susan and Mr Brown.

'Were we all right?' asked Susan as soon as she saw her mother and brother.

'You were wonderful – both of you!' said Mrs Brown – and she meant it.

'Thanks for your help, Hamlet,' said Susan. 'I don't know what I'd have done without you.'

'It was nothing,' said Hamlet.

'Not so, my boy!' boomed Mr Brown. 'It

was everything! In the theatre every part is important, however tiny it may seem to be. Today Susan played her part and played it beautifully — but you, Hamlet, you played your part as well. I was proud of you both, as proud as proud could be!'

Mr Brown peeled off his long false beard and turned to his wife. 'We are very lucky to have two such clever children, aren't we, my dear?' he said.

'Hic!' said Mrs Brown. 'Hic! Hic!'

Mrs Brown should not have rushed that hot dog. She should not have gulped that coffee. Mrs Brown had the hiccups — and everybody laughed.

More Young Puffins

THE GHOST AT NO. 13
Gyles Brandreth

Hamlet Brown's sister, Susan, is just too perfect. Everything she does is praised and Hamlet is in despair – until a ghost comes to stay for a holiday and helps him to find an exciting idea for his school project!

RADIO DETECTIVE
John Escott

A piece of amazing deduction by the Roundbay Radio Detective when Donald, the radio's young presenter, solves a mystery but finds out more than anyone expects.

RAGDOLLY ANNA'S CIRCUS
Jean Kenward

Made only from a morsel of this and a tatter of that, Ragdolly Anna is a very special doll and the six stories in this book are all about her adventures.

SEE YOU AT THE MATCH
Margaret Joy

Six delightful stories about football. Whether spectator, player, winner or loser these short, easy stories for young readers are a must for all football fans.

THE RAILWAY CAT'S SECRET

Phyllis Arkle

Stories about Alfie, the Railway Cat, and his sworn enemy Hack the porter. Alfie tries to win over Hack by various means with often hilarious results.

WORD PARTY

Richard Edwards

A delightful collection of poems – lively, snappy and easy to read.

THE THREE AND MANY WISHES OF JASON REID

Hazel Hutchins

Jason is eleven and a very good thinker so when he is granted three wishes he is very wary indeed. After all, he knows the tangles that happen in fairy stories!

THE AIR-RAID SHELTER

Jeremy Strong

Adam and his sister Rachel find a perfect place for their secret camp in the grounds of a deserted house, until they are discovered by their sworn enemies and things go from bad to worse.

UPSIDE DOWN STORIES

Donald Bisset

Brilliant nonsense tales to delight children, telling about such oddities as an inexperienced apple tree which grows squirrels instead of apples!

DORRIE AND THE BIRTHDAY EGGS

Patricia Coombs

When the eggs for the Big Witch's birthday cake get broken by mistake, Dorrie sets off to buy some more from the Egg Witch. But her errand takes her through the forest, and lurking there is Thinnever Vetch, all ready to make mischief . . .

ALLOTMENT LANE SCHOOL AGAIN

Margaret Joy

It's always fun in Miss Mee's class and now the holidays are over and everyone is glad to be back at Allotment Lane School again. Fourteen lively stories about Class 1 and their friends.

HANK PRANK AND HOT HENRIETTA

Jules Older

Hank and his hot-tempered sister, Henrietta, are always getting themselves into trouble but the doings of this terrible pair make for an entertaining series of adventures.